KU-761-000

Tiana

The Grand Opening

This edition published by Parragon in 2012
Parragon
Queen Street House
4 Queen Street
Bath BA1 1HE, UK
www.parragon.com

Copyright © 2012 Disney Enterprises, Inc
The movie THE PRINCESS AND THE FROG Copyright © 2009 Disney, story
inspired in part by the book THE FROG PRINCESS by E.D. Baker Copyright ©
2002, published by Bloomsbury Publishing, Inc.

All rights reserved. No part of this publication may be reproduced, stored
in a retrieval system or transmitted, in any form or by any means, electronic,
mechanical, photocopying, recording or otherwise, without the prior
permission of the copyright holder.

ISBN 978-1-4454-9668-9
Printed in China

Tiana
The Grand Opening

By Helen Perelman
Illustrated by Studio IBOIX
and Dave Courtland

PaRragon

Bath · New York · Singapore · Hong Kong · Cologne · Delhi
Melbourne · Amsterdam · Johannesburg · Shenzhen

Chapter One

$\mathcal{P}$rincess Tiana twirled around her new palace. It may not have been the palace of every princess's dreams, but she loved it. She and Prince Naveen had worked hard to turn an old sugar mill into a brand-new restaurant called Tiana's Palace. Tiana gazed up at the large chandelier in the grand room and let out a happy sigh. She had dreamed about this her entire life.

When Tiana fell in love with Naveen, he had been a frog prince. And he'd turned her into a frog, too! While they were in the bayou, she never thought that they would get married, turn back into humans and open a New Orleans restaurant together. Tiana looked over at her prince and smiled.

"Naveen, everything is perfect!" she cried. "The chandelier was the last touch." For years, Tiana had thought the rundown mill would make the perfect spot for a restaurant. She looked around. After a couple of months making repairs, everything looked beautiful.

"This is just the kind of restaurant I always wanted," Tiana said to Naveen. She sat down at one of the tables in the spacious room and gazed at the new dining area.

The tables had golden tablecloths and napkins. It was all fit for a princess!

"When Daddy and I used to talk about opening a restaurant, this is what I hoped it would be like," she said. "Thank you!"

"You've done all the work!" Naveen exclaimed. "Without your dedication, this place would still be an old sugar mill. And if it wasn't for your delicious food, no one would want to eat here!"

"Oh, the people will come to hear your music," Tiana added with a smile.

Naveen loved jazz music. He played the ukulele and had a wonderful singing voice. One of their best friends was a musician named Louis, who also happened to be an alligator!

Tiana and Naveen had met Louis in the bayou when they were both frogs. He played the trumpet better than anyone they knew. "Without you and Louis, Tiana's Palace wouldn't be as much fun. The Firefly Five is the best jazz band in New Orleans!"

"Good food, good music and good friends," Naveen said. "I think that is the recipe for a successful restaurant."

Tiana looked down at her hands. "Everyone has been very kind, but we haven't even had our grand opening yet. The first night is a big deal."

"Especially if Jono La Crème is coming!" Charlotte LaBouff called as she walked into the room. She and Tiana had grown up together and were best friends.

Charlotte's blonde hair was perfectly styled, and she wore a beautiful purple silk dress. Waving a letter, she rushed over to Tiana's table. "Y'all are not going to believe this delicious news!" she exclaimed as she sat down next to Tiana. Her blue eyes sparkled. She was bursting with excitement.

"Lottie," Tiana said, "What on earth are you up to?"

"She definitely looks as if she's up to something," Naveen agreed, nodding his head.

Charlotte took a moment to enjoy watching her friends. She was so excited! Her news was so big she could hardly speak.

"Tell us!" Tiana pleaded.

"Well," Charlotte finally began. She smoothed her fancy dress with her hands. She batted her eyelashes, then slowly exhaled. Finally she spat out her news in one breath: "Daddy was talking to friends of his, and someone knew someone who knew someone else, and that man knows Jono La Crème!"

Tiana screamed. She grabbed Charlotte's hands. The two friends started to jump up and down.

"Who is Jono La Crème?" Naveen asked, slightly bewildered. He was from Maldonia, not New Orleans like Tiana and Charlotte.

Laughing, Charlotte fanned herself with the letter. "Jono La Crème is only the most well-respected food critic in the South!" she exclaimed.

"If he gives you a good review in his newspaper column, Crème de La Crème, you are a guaranteed success!" Tiana added. She turned to Charlotte. "Is he really coming here?" Her eyes widened. "He's coming to *my* restaurant?"

"Yes, ma'am," Charlotte said, grinning. "For opening night!"

Naveen rubbed his chin. "Wait, I think that I've read some of his articles. His reviews can get spicier than a bowl of jambalaya!"

"But he is going to love Tiana's Palace," Charlotte said confidently. "When he tastes your gumbo and beignets, he'll be in food heaven. He's from New Orleans, after all." She handed the letter to Tiana.

Tiana studied it. The stationery was beautiful. Jono La Crème's penmanship was very neat. Tiana quickly read the note. "He really is coming here!" she exclaimed. She grabbed Charlotte's hands again and swung her around in a circle. "Oh, Lottie," she said. "Thank you!"

"It's wonderful news, isn't it?" Charlotte said, feeling very proud. "I want everyone to know about Tiana's Palace!"

Naveen clapped. "Bravo, Charlotte," he said. "A good review is the best advertising for a restaurant."

Suddenly, Tiana stopped dancing. She sank back down in her chair.

"Wait," she said, catching her breath. "What if Jono La Crème doesn't like my food?" she asked. The smile disappeared from her face.

"Don't be silly," Charlotte said. She waved her arm around. "He'll love this place – and you, Princess Tiana!"

Tiana shook her head. "If Jono La Crème is coming here for the opening, we have to make sure everything is perfect. We can't have any mistakes."

"I thought you'd say that," Charlotte replied. Tiana had always been a hard worker. "And I'm here to help in any way that I can." Charlotte reached out to give her good friend a hug.

"You can count on me, too," Naveen said. "Though you have nothing to worry about. That man is in for a heaping plate of good Southern cooking!"

"And the best part," Charlotte continued, "is he loves jazz music! Wait until he hears Naveen and Louis play."

"Opening night is going to be a grand party," Naveen said. He gave Tiana's hand a squeeze.

Tiana nodded. She just hoped that they could get everything done in time. New menus, decorations, music – there were so many details!

Chapter Two

The week leading up to opening night was very busy. Tiana carefully planned the menu and even tried a few new recipes. She met with the florist and picked out the most colourful flowers for the centrepieces. All the silver was polished, and the table-cloths were cleaned and pressed. Tiana's Palace sparkled, from the new chandelier to the silverware on the tables.

The morning of the opening, Tiana was in the kitchen before the sun came up. She was going to spend the day cooking and preparing for the big event. She wanted to get an early start!

Music from the dining room floated into the kitchen. Tiana knew that she wasn't the only one getting ready for the opening. Naveen, Louis and the other musicians were practicing. They had no reason to worry, Tiana thought. They sounded fantastic!

Dicing her vegetables to the beat of the music, she hummed along. The food that night had to be the very best.

The morning passed quickly, and soon it was lunchtime. The band members strolled into the kitchen. One of the perks of working at Tiana's Palace was that they got to eat there.

"Something smells delicious in here," Naveen said as he swung open the door. He sniffed around the kitchen and walked over to a large pot simmering on the stove. He lifted the lid and took a peek. "Mmmm, this is going to be divine!"

"Thank you," Tiana said, wiping her hands on her apron. "I sure hope Jono likes it."

"You have nothing to be nervous about," Louis said as he strolled into the kitchen. "Listen, I wrote this song for you." He did a quick scat on his trumpet.

The song made Tiana sway to the beat and forget to be nervous. The jazz tune was so catchy it made her smile.

"I love that song," Tiana said. "Will you play it tonight?"

"Of course!" Louis replied. "Giselle has never let me down, and your cooking won't either." He patted his trumpet. "Tiana, you are the best cook in New Orleans, and Jono La Crème is gonna love this place."

Tiana hugged Louis. He was a true friend. She pulled back and smiled up at him, realizing he was also a very tall friend!

"Louis, could you reach that large red pot on the top shelf?" she asked. She pointed to the far end of the kitchen. "I need to make jambalaya and want to use the biggest pot I have."

"Sure thing," Louis said. He was more than happy to help out Tiana. He easily reached the heavy pot and put it down on the stove. "Just save me some of that jambalaya!" He licked his lips. "And some gumbo, étouffée, bread pudding and a plateful of beignets!"

"Promise," Tiana said, smiling. Then she spotted the kitchen clock and gasped. "I didn't realize the time! I've got to get down to the French Market. I need to have the freshest fish today."

"I can go for you," Naveen offered.

"Are you sure?" Tiana asked. "You wouldn't mind?"

"Not at all, Princess," her prince replied.

"I can go with you," Louis said. "I tend to clear a crowd. That way we can get to the fish place quickly." He swayed his head and giggled.

"That would be fantastic," Naveen said. "I'll need a hand with the shipment. If I know Tiana, she ordered enough fish for an entire kingdom!" He smiled at his wife.

"I would appreciate that very much," Tiana told them. "There should be one large crate of fish. Murray the fisherman was going to put aside the best selection for me."

"We'll go now," Naveen said. He touched Tiana on the arm. "Tonight is going to be great."

Tiana went back to chopping her vegetables. She only looked up when there was a knock at the back door. "What are you doing here so early?" Tiana exclaimed when she saw who was standing there.

Her mother, Eudora, gave her a tight squeeze. "When Lottie told me the news, I had to come over right away," she said. "Jono La Crème, coming here? I wanted to help if I could."

"Everything is happening so quickly," Tiana said. "And I want the evening to be perfect."

Touching Tiana's cheek, her mother smiled. "One ingredient at a time," she said, "just like your daddy taught you."

Tiana was glad her mother had come early. Having her in the kitchen would help Tiana focus on her cooking.

"I brought you something," Eudora said. She drew a large box from her bag. "For your opening night."

Tiana pulled a beautiful blue silk dress with sparkles all over it out of the box. Her mother was an amazing seamstress, so she always knew just what to make. "This is beautiful," she murmured.

"Fit for a princess, don't you think?" her mother said with a smile. "I made the dress especially for you. There's something else in there as well. Look."

Tiana dug deeper into the box and pulled out a crisp, white apron trimmed with bows and a ruffle. "Mama, it's gorgeous! I love it!"

She slipped the apron on. "This is just the thing for opening night. Thank you for everything, and for being here today."

"I wouldn't have missed this night for anything!" she exclaimed, kissing the top of Tiana's head. "You know your father would be so proud of you."

Tiana's face grew serious. "Do you think that Jono La Crème will like my food?"

"I have no doubt," Eudora said. "And he'll love this restaurant. It's like your father always said, 'Food brings folks together from all walks of life. It warms them right up and puts smiles on their faces.'"

Suddenly, Tiana smelled something burning. She had forgotten that her jambalaya was on the stove! She raced over to the pot. "Oh, heavens!" she cried. "Where is my head?" She whisked the pot off the stove.

"Babycakes," her mother said calmly. "You've got to concentrate on one thing at a time."

Tiana blew a strand of hair off her forehead. "Whew, that was close!" She sighed. "I can't go serving Mr La Crème burned jambalaya!"

"You are going to be fine," her mother told her.

"Thank you," Tiana said.

Together, Tiana and her mother made some new jambalaya, prepared the roux for her special gumbo and whipped up some skillet corn bread.

A while later, Louis and Naveen returned. They were lugging a crate filled with ice and fish.

"Royal delivery!" Naveen shouted as they entered the kitchen.

"Nothing like the smell of fresh fish!" Louis said, grinning. "Reminds me of when I was just a little gator back in the bayou."

"Hello, Louis," Eudora said, waving. "I'm looking forward to hearing your music."

Louis nodded his large head. "Giselle and I are going to play some sweet jazz for the crowd."

Suddenly, Louis's eyes grew wide. "Wait!" he shouted. "Where is Giselle?" He looked down at his empty hands. Then he spun around, his large tail just missing the pot on the stove.

Everyone in the kitchen froze. Louis was never without his trumpet. "I can't play on opening night without Giselle!"

Chapter Three

"Let's try to calm down," Tiana said to Louis. She didn't like to see her friend so upset. She took a seat at the long wooden table in the kitchen. Pointing to a chair nearby, she said, "Why don't you sit down? Take some deep breaths."

"I can't play without my Giselle!" Louis wailed. He made his way over and slumped in the chair. "Oh, this is terrible!" He looked over at Tiana sadly. "I'm going to ruin opening night for you!"

Tiana and Naveen shared a look. They weren't sure what to do. Naveen gave Tiana an encouraging nod.

"We will find Giselle," Tiana told him.

"You can be sure of that," Naveen said, standing beside Louis.

"You had Giselle earlier today when you played that new song for me here in the kitchen," Tiana said encouragingly. "Remember?"

Louis sniffled and nodded his head.

"We're all worrying too much about the grand opening," Tiana said. "I almost burned the jambalaya this morning!"

Eudora stood beside Louis. "Tiana's right. Let's try to be calm." She smiled kindly at the sad alligator. "I always find it best to retrace my steps when I can't find something."

Tiana nodded. "Louis, did you take Giselle to the market with you?"

Louis scratched his head.

"I don't think you had Giselle with you," Naveen said thoughtfully.

Louis grew more upset. "Oh, I don't

know!" he cried. A tear slid down his face. "But I do know that I can't play without her!" He put his head in his hands.

"Let's try to figure this out," Tiana said gently. "When was the last time you remember seeing Giselle?"

Louis shook his head. "The last time I remember seeing her was when I was in the kitchen, here with you," he told Tiana. "That was before we went to the market for the fish."

"Okay, so let's check the kitchen!" Tiana exclaimed. "Everyone, search everywhere! The trumpet must be here."

Tiana, Naveen, Eudora and Louis looked in every corner of the kitchen.

But no one found the shiny golden trumpet.

Louis wagged his head. "I'm sorry, Tiana," he said sadly. He wiped the tears from his eyes. "I just can't play tonight without Giselle."

"Maybe I should check the market," Naveen offered. "I know Louis didn't have Giselle on the way home, but I'm not sure that he didn't have her when we went there." He looked over at his sad pal. "It's worth a try."

Tiana glanced at Louis. She didn't really have time to spare. But she knew how much the trumpet meant to her friend. "I'll go with you, Naveen," she said. Before anyone could stop them, Tiana and Naveen were off to the French Market.

Jackson Square was bustling with people

shopping and enjoying the warm afternoon. Naveen carefully retraced the steps he had taken on his errand. "We walked down this street," he explained. "And then cut across to the market over here." He pointed to a wide street that led down to the water.

"I'll take this side of the street," Tiana said. "And you take the other."

"Poor Louis," Naveen said. "I'm not sure how I'd feel if I lost my ukulele."

Tiana gave Naveen's hand a squeeze. "We're going to find Giselle. We have to!" Then she crossed the street.

As Tiana searched, she walked up behind two fancy ladies. When she tried to get past them, Tiana overheard their conversation.

"Frieda, are you going to the opening of

Tiana's Palace tonight?" the woman in the purple hat asked.

"Yes," Frieda responded. "We were lucky enough to get reservations."

"You *are* lucky!" her friend exclaimed. She leaned in a little closer. "You know, I heard an alligator is going to play in the jazz band there." She raised her hand to her chest dramatically. "They say he's the best trumpet player you'll ever hear!"

Tiana tried not to laugh out loud. If only Louis could hear these ladies talking about him and his music!

"Yes," the woman went on. "I know it sounds crazy, but he's fantastic. I heard him play during Mardi Gras. He had the most soulful sound. I loved listening to his music!"

During Mardi Gras, Louis's dream of playing on one of the floats in the parade had come true.

Now Tiana wanted Louis to play at the grand opening more than ever! She quickly passed the two ladies and sped over to the fish stall where Naveen and Louis had gotten the fish.

No Giselle.

"Do you think Giselle will turn up?" Tiana called to Naveen as they walked.

He walked over to her. "I really hope so," he said. "I wouldn't want Tiana's Palace to open without Louis's music."

"We'll find her," Tiana said.

The sky was growing dark as the sun began to sink lower in the sky.

With heavy hearts, Naveen and Tiana went back to the restaurant.

Chapter Four

Louis was sitting outside Tiana's Palace, waiting for Tiana and Naveen. He leapt up when he saw them coming. Then he noticed their sad faces. He knew that they hadn't found his trumpet. His tail flopped on the ground.

"I'm so sorry," Tiana said to Louis. "We looked everywhere."

"Maybe we should check inside again," Naveen said.

"It's no use," Louis said. "Maybe it just wasn't meant to be." Covering his eyes with his arm, he tried to hide his sad face.

Tiana rushed to his side. "Louis, you can't give up hope!" she exclaimed. "Remember when Naveen and I were frogs? If we had given up hope, we never would have made it here. You need to have some faith."

Naveen took his cue from Tiana and chimed in. "Louis, please come inside," he said.

Louis raised his head. "It's late, Tiana. You need to get back to your cooking," he told her. He sniffled. "I'll be fine. Please go back to the kitchen. If Jono La Crème comes and there is no food on his plate, then the night will truly be a disaster!"

"I'll stay here with him," Naveen told Tiana. "You go inside and start the gumbo."

Even though she didn't want to leave, Tiana knew that she had to get back to cooking. "I'll keep searching," Tiana said. "Giselle has got to show up!"

Back inside her kitchen, Tiana took a deep breath. She looked under the table and by the shelves in a corner of the room. These were places she had checked before, but she remembered seeing Louis and Giselle there.

Her mother came over to her. "Tiana, the time!" she exclaimed. "You need to get that gumbo on the stove." She pointed to the kitchen clock. "Lottie will be here soon to help you get ready. And you still have a few dishes to prepare!"

Tiana glanced over at the counter where her father's old gumbo pot was sitting.

Nothing meant more to Tiana than having that pot in her restaurant. She had so many memories of cooking with her dad. She remembered the joy he had gotten from watching friends and family enjoy his food.

Tiana knew that was the heart of her restaurant. Even if there was no music, she would still serve up good food. She took the pot in her hands and hugged it tight.

Glancing down, she saw a glimmer of gold. She let out a scream. Naveen and Louis came rushing into the kitchen.

"Giselle!" Tiana cried. She held up the trumpet in her hand. "Louis, you put her in my father's gumbo pot!"

Louis leaped towards Tiana, nearly toppling some cooling beignets. He hugged the instrument and then played a song. Tiana recognized it as the one that he had played earlier.

"You must have put her down when I asked you to get the pot," Tiana said. She smiled at Louis. "I guess that was a pretty safe place."

Naveen laughed. "You mean a *secret* place!" He slapped Louis playfully on his back. "Glad that you have reunited with Giselle. You are the perfect pair."

"And now y'all need to leave," Tiana teased. "I have some cooking to do here."

Louis bowed his head. "Thank you, Tiana," he said. "And Giselle and I would be pleased as punch to play tonight. In fact, we're going to play some new songs. We're going to show Jono La Crème a good old New Orleans time!"

Tiana loved the sound of that! "A party fit for a princess and a prince?" she kidded as she shooed Louis and Naveen out the door.

"Yes!" Louis exclaimed.

Tiana was feeling good about the night, even though she'd had a couple of mishaps. She threw some ingredients into the pot – one at a time, just as her mum had advised. Everything was going to be fine. That is, if she got that gumbo going! The doors to the restaurant would open in a couple of hours, and she had a lot to do.

Chapter Five

*A*s the evening stars appeared in the night sky, Tiana was bustling around the kitchen. Her hair was twisted up in a fancy bun on top of her head. The dress her mother had made for her fit perfectly. Her fancy apron shielded her from any splats or spurts from the pots simmering on the stove.

Louis was playing his beloved trumpet in the dining room, along with Naveen and the band. Once again, Tiana hummed happily. She felt like a princess in her palace. And tonight it was as if the ball she had always dreamed about would finally happen.

"Why, it smells and sounds like a grand ole party in here!" Charlotte said as she burst into the kitchen.

Tiana looked over at her good friend. Charlotte was wearing a pink dress that looked delicious enough to eat. "You look beautiful, Lottie!" Tiana called. "I love your dress!"

"My favourite dressmaker and sous-chef made this for me," Charlotte said, beaming at Tiana's mother.

Eudora laughed and looked down at her hands. "Yes, if I'm not sewing, then I'm chopping vegetables!" she said, laughing.

She blew Charlotte a kiss and then turned her attention back to her work.

"Daddy is already at our table," Charlotte said to Tiana. She gestured to the dining room. "But I had to come in and see you! I'm so excited about your grand opening."

"Me, too," Tiana gushed. "It's been a crazy day, but now I think we're all set."

Charlotte peered under a cloth on the counter. She licked her lips when she saw what was underneath.

"Can I sample of one the princess's famous beignets?" she asked. The freshly fried dough squares sprinkled with powdered sugar were too tempting!

Tiana laughed. "Sure," she said. "Help yourself!"

"Oh, these are simply the best!" Charlotte declared.

As Tiana watched her friend enjoy the treat, she couldn't help but sigh. Leaning against the counter, she checked her list of things to do for opening night. "I can't believe it – we're right on schedule," she told her friend. "I've been checking my list, and everything is going well. Now we just have to wait for Jono La Crème to arrive."

Licking the sugar off her fingers, Charlotte nodded. "I had no doubt that you'd have a schedule. You've always had a plan, Tiana. And that plan involved opening this very restaurant. Don't worry, Jono is going to love this place. It'll be the best party New Orleans has seen since Mardi Gras!"

She spun around joyfully, accidentally knocking the plateful of beignets to the floor.

"Oh, sugar sticks!" Charlotte cried. "Look what I've done!" She bent down to gather up the beignets. "I'm so sorry, Tiana! Now you won't have any beignets for opening night."

Tiana patted her friend's arm. "Don't worry," she said. "I think I still have time to make some more. Nothing is going to ruin this night!"

She tossed the fallen beignets in the garbage. "I'm concentrating on one thing at a time. All the food is being warmed up. The music is playing, and friends are arriving."

But Tiana was worried. What else could

go wrong? she wondered.

Just then, the kitchen door swung open.
Naveen entered with his parents, the king
and queen of Maldonia. Tiana rushed over
to greet her in-laws with a formal bow, but
they both reached out to give her a hug.

"We're thrilled to be here," the king said, grinning. "I've been dreaming of your gumbo our whole trip."

"And your delicious corn bread," the queen added. "Everything looks wonderful, Tiana. Well done!"

Tiana blushed. "Thank you for coming. This night means so much to me, and to Naveen. He and the band have prepared a special song in your honour."

Naveen nodded. "Yes, it's true," he said. "We've come up with a few new numbers for this evening. We hope that you'll dance and enjoy."

Lottie clapped her hands together and did a little jump. "I am just so excited to be here for this party."

"Come out and greet our guests," Naveen said, taking Tiana's hand. "You should see all the people. Everyone is anxious to meet the princess behind the food!"

He saw Tiana's eyes flash.

"No, Jono La Crème isn't here yet," he said, assuring her. "But don't worry, he'll have a great time – and a great meal – once he arrives."

Tiana followed Naveen, his parents and Lottie out the door. The dining room looked beautiful. The golden tablecloths glistened in the warm light of the chandelier. The lilies and birds-of-paradise smelled wonderful. And the delicious aroma from the kitchen wafted through the room. Tiana smiled and greeted her guests.

"Tia!" someone shouted from across the room. A girl came rushing towards Tiana.

"Georgia!" Tiana blurted out. She hugged her friend tightly. "I'm so glad you came!"

Georgia smiled. "Girl, you know I never miss a good party," she said, grinning. Her short curly hair was styled in a bob, and her purple and black dress fitted her perfectly. "Tia, this place is gorgeous," she gushed. "You've come a long way from waiting tables at Duke's Diner!"

Smiling, Tiana thanked her old friend. When Tiana was first starting out, she had worked double shifts waiting tables in restaurants. She had big dreams but no money. While Georgia and many of her friends were out on the town, Tiana always had to work. She was thankful that her hard work had paid off, and that she could share this opening night with her old and new friends.

"Enjoy," Tiana told Georgia.

"I will, My Royal Highness . . . I mean, Your Royal Highness!" Georgia said, giggling. Then she said, "I still can't get used to that."

"I can't either!" Tiana responded. She touched the tiara on her head and moved on to the next table to greet more guests.

Just at that moment, the lights flickered. Tiana looked up, and in a flash, the lights in the chandelier flicked off.

An opening-night blackout?

That was not on the menu!

Chapter Six

Tiana took a deep breath. Instead of seeing the golden glow of the chandelier in the dining room, all she saw was darkness. Her heart began to race. What happened? she thought. Everything was going so well!

"Sorry about that," Tiana announced to the restaurant guests. "We'll get everything sorted out before you know it."

In an instant, Naveen was at Tiana's side. He squeezed her hand and escorted her back to the kitchen. "We'll fix this," he whispered in her ear. "Remember, we've been in worse situations!"

Lottie and Georgia came through the kitchen door, holding candles. "Whatever happened, we're here to help," Lottie said.

Her mother walked over, holding a candle. "Are all the lights out?"

"Yes," Tiana answered. "But we're going to get this fixed in no time. We have to make sure the candles on all the tables are lit." She was grateful for the tall golden candelabras with four long, tapered candles on each table. At least people wouldn't be sitting in the dark!

Lottie, Georgia and Tiana's mother grabbed some matches and went to light up the dining room.

"Tell Louis to start playing," Tiana called after Lottie. "Music will keep everyone calm."

"I'll tell him," Lottie promised.

Tiana turned to face Naveen. "Maybe this has something to do with the new chandelier?" she said.

"I'll check on that," Naveen said. "Do you want to make sure that there are enough candles?"

Holding up a candle to light her way, Tiana went into the storage closet.

Of all the nights for this to happen, she thought. What a royal mess!

"The food is all ready," Eudora said to her daughter. "And it will stay hot on the gas stove!" She peered out the kitchen door. "You know, Tia, the dining room looks beautiful in candlelight. Maybe this isn't such a bad thing."

Tiana wasn't so sure about that. She was sure Jono La Crème was expecting to see a well-lit restaurant. What would he report about a dark dining room? She hung her head.

"Maybe the chandelier was a bad idea," she said glumly. "I just thought it would really make this place into a palace, you know?" She sank down into one of the kitchen chairs.

Her mother sat beside her. "It *is* a palace," her mum said.

Tiana looked up at her mother. All of the problems that day had finally got to her. "Thanks," she mumbled. "But I don't feel so royal now. I wanted everything to be perfect for the opening and to impress Jono La Crème."

Shaking her head, Eudora laughed. "Oh, Tiana," she said, "you don't need to impress anyone. Remember that your dream was to open a restaurant so other people could enjoy your food. You have a gift – just like your father did."

Tiana's shoulders were still slumped. Her sparkly tiara slipped off her head and clunked down on the table.

"I have two people working on the lighting problem. It looks like a fuse blew," Naveen reported as he came into the kitchen.

When he noticed that Tiana was looking sad, he went to her and draped his arm around her shoulders. "Don't worry, we'll get this fixed in no time." He smiled at her. "I promise."

Tiana wanted to believe Naveen, but she couldn't help feeling sad. "First Louis loses his trumpet, and now this! What next?"

"Come here," Naveen said, holding out his hand. He guided Tiana over to the window and pointed outside. "Look up at the stars," he told her. "Remember how you once wished on a star?"

Tiana nodded her head. How could she forget? That was the night she had met Naveen.

"You have your restaurant and so much more. This is just one small problem. It'll be just fine." Naveen grinned. "Now can we please have some of your amazing gumbo?"

"Thanks, Naveen," Tiana whispered.

Eudora came up behind them. "And no one would be prouder of you than your father," she added. "In candlelight or in the light of a fancy chandelier."

Tiana nodded. She had a restaurant full of people and a kitchen full of food. If this was her dream, she had better start serving it up!

"You're right," she said. "But what will Jono La Crème think?" She looked at Naveen and her mother. "Big Daddy got him to come, and I don't want to disappoint him."

"You'll find out soon enough," Charlotte said, sneaking up on them. "Mr La Crème just walked in! He's sitting at a table right now."

"Oh, no!" Tiana said in a panic.

"Oh, he's peachy keen," Charlotte explained. "The maître d' escorted him to his table with a candle in his hand. He seems very happy. He's already tapping his fingers to Louis's music."

Tiana turned to Naveen. "You better get out there and play!" she said. "Louis will be wondering where you are. I'll be all right, I promise."

Lottie went over to the table and picked up the tiara. "Here, Tia," she said. "Now go introduce yourself to your newest guest. I just know he is looking forward to meeting you."

A smile spread across Tiana's face. As she put on the tiara, the lights flickered back on.

Naveen gave Tiana a quick kiss on her cheek. Then he held up his ukulele. "Now I am off to play a good old piece of jazz."

Tiana smiled and walked out of the kitchen to meet the famous Mr Jono La Crème.

Chapter Seven

From across the room, Tiana saw Jono La Crème. He was sitting at a table near the front of the restaurant. He wore a pin-striped brown suit with a white shirt and a yellow tie. He was mostly bald with a little bit of dark hair, and he had a small moustache that curled up at the ends. His large belly spilled over his pants. Tiana thought he definitely looked like a man who loved food.

"Go ahead." Charlotte had seen her friend hesitate. She gave Tiana a little push forwards. "Introduce yourself to him." She smiled warmly. "He's going to rave about your food; don't worry so much!"

Tiana walked slowly towards the table. As she got closer, she saw that next to Mr La Crème was a pad of paper and a pen. What would he write? Would he tell people to come to her restaurant?

Tiana took a deep breath and walked up to Mr La Crème. Charlotte was still standing across the room, watching. She waved encouragingly.

Tiana waited until the song ended. Charlotte was right about Mr La Crème liking music. He seemed to be enjoying the band. When Louis blew a long note to end the song, Tiana walked up to the critic.

"Welcome to Tiana's Palace, Mr La Crème," she said boldly. She extended her hand. "I am Tiana, and I'm so glad that you could be with us this evening."

Her heart was racing! She was trying to sound calm, but she wondered if he could tell how nervous she was to have him in her restaurant.

"Lovely to meet you, Princess," he said in a slow Southern drawl. "I'm looking forward to tasting your food. The LaBouffs speak very highly of you." He leaned back in his chair and sniffed the air. "Something in that kitchen of yours smells good."

"Well, I sure hope you enjoy the food,"

she said. She backed away and scurried into the kitchen. Her mother was loading up the tray for Mr La Crème. A waiter was standing by to take the food to him, but Tiana put her hand up.

"I'd like to take this tray," she said.

Her mother smiled at her. "I'm sure Mr La Crème would like that," she said sweetly.

Tiana carried a tray with her gumbo, a basket of homemade biscuits and skillet corn bread. She placed the dishes on the table in front of Mr La Crème.

"I was raised on my granddaddy's gumbo," Mr La Crème told her. He opened his napkin and tucked it into his collar. "But I'm looking forward to trying yours."

Tiana smiled. "Thank you," she said. "The recipe is my daddy's, and it was passed down to him. I hope you have a great time here tonight. Please enjoy."

As she walked back to the kitchen, Tiana wasn't sure what to think. Would Mr La

Crème like the gumbo? Was it too spicy? Not spicy enough? Knowing that he grew up with a favourite gumbo worried Tiana. She ducked into the kitchen and then peered through the small round window in the door.

Charlotte and Tiana's mother also tried to get a glimpse of Mr La Crème. The three of them wondered what he was thinking.

First, Mr La Crème sniffed the gumbo. Then he took his spoon and made swirls in the bowl. After a few moments, he lifted a spoonful up to his nose.

"Oh, the suspense!" Charlotte cried.

"Heavens!" Tiana's mother said. She wiped her forehead with a handkerchief. "I wish he'd taste the food already!"

"I know," Tiana said with a heavy sigh. "I wish he would eat!"

As soon as the spoon hit Mr La Crème's lips, Tiana got a huge surprise! The kitchen door flung open and pushed her, Charlotte and her mother clear across the room!

"Oh, no!" Naveen cried. "Are you all right?" He hurried towards them. One at a time, he helped them up. When they were all standing, he looked at them inquisitively. "What were you doing there, anyway?"

Tiana blushed. She was embarrassed to admit that she'd been trying to spy on the food critic. "We were just trying to get a glimpse of Mr La Crème as he tried my gumbo," she said sheepishly. She felt silly getting caught. She looked up at Naveen.

"The fate of this restaurant is in his hands," she blurted out.

"You mean his mouth," Charlotte said, giggling. She ran over and peered through the door again. She started to jump up and down. "Now he's trying the biscuits!"

Naveen grabbed Tiana's hand. "*Ma cherie*, he is one person. You are worrying about him too much. Come and dance with me."

"Wait a second," Charlotte shouted. "He's fixin' to leave! He's talking to my daddy at the next table and heading for the door."

"Do you think that he didn't like the food?" Tiana asked. She ran to the door to try and see what was going on. "What about the dessert? We have some delicious bread pudding and my beignets!"

Charlotte shook her head. "I know!" she cried. "I'll give him some dessert to take home!" She gathered a couple of Tiana's famous beignets and packed them in a red-and-white chequered napkin and ran out of the kitchen.

Tiana hung her head. After all that work, La Crème hadn't even stayed to finish his dinner.

Suddenly, she saw Naveen holding out his hand.

"Dance with me," he said again. "Dance with me on opening night at Tiana's Palace, the best restaurant in New Orleans."

Tiana took her prince's hand and walked out to the dining room. She didn't feel much like dancing.

But when Louis and the Firefly Five played a ballad, she began to feel better.

All around her were people she loved and cared about. And they were there because of the good food and music. That's what Tiana's Palace was all about.

As Naveen twirled her around the floor, she couldn't help but smile. At that moment, she didn't care what Jono La Crème wrote. This was her dream come true. She was surrounded by what was most important – love.

She laughed as Naveen dipped her on the final note of the song. No matter what Jono La Crème wrote, this night had turned into a recipe for success!

Chapter Eight

The next morning, Tiana awoke before the sun was up. She couldn't sleep! The celebration at Tiana's Palace had been so much fun. Everyone in town had been there and had a good time.

But today she would get to read the review that Jono La Crème had written. Even though he left early, Tiana hoped he had enjoyed himself.

Tiana got to the restaurant just as the sun was rising. To her surprise, her mother, Charlotte and Naveen were already in the kitchen waiting for her.

"I guess none of us could wait for the morning paper," Charlotte said, smiling. "Lord knows this is the earliest I've gotten up in a while."

"I'll make some café au lait," Tiana's mother offered.

"I'll make some beignets," Tiana said.

"I was hoping you'd say that!" Naveen exclaimed.

"Me, too!" Charlotte chimed in.

Tiana was happy she didn't have to wait alone for the paper to arrive. Even though she'd had a wonderful time last night, she still couldn't wait to see what Mr La Crème had to say about her food.

"Mr La Crème left so quickly last night," Tiana said. She stirred the batter. "I couldn't tell if he liked the gumbo."

"How could he not like your gumbo?" Naveen asked. "You pour your heart and soul into your food. A man like that has to know that makes the difference."

Tiana plopped the dough in the oil to fry. "Oh, let's hope," she said.

"You know, this is just the kind of place your daddy wanted for you," her mother said, giving her a hug. "It's truly a palace."

"A palace of good food, good friends and good music!" Louis bellowed. He stuck his head in the door. "Good morning!"

Tiana ran over to Louis. She gave the alligator a big hug. "Thank you for all that great music last night," she gushed. "I loved all the new songs. You kept everyone's feet tapping. Thank you."

Louis bowed his head. "It was my pleasure," he said. "I had a grand time." He reached behind his back. "And I thought you'd like this." In his hand, Louis had the morning paper!

"Hot off the press!" Naveen called.

Tiana looked at the newspaper. She wanted to know what Jono La Crème had written, but she was too nervous to read the review! She looked up at Naveen.

"I'll read it," Naveen said. He could tell that Tiana was anxious.

He took it over to the large wooden kitchen table. He opened it and scanned the pages for the La Crème de La Crème section. "Ah, here it is!" Naveen exclaimed. He pointed to a column at the top of the page.

Everyone rushed over to stand near as Naveen read the review. Only Tiana stayed where she was, making the beignets. She had to keep busy. She was too nervous to stand still and listen!

"'Last night, I ate at the new Tiana's Palace. The gumbo didn't taste like my granddaddy's,'" Naveen read.

Oh, no! Tiana thought. He really didn't like her gumbo! She stopped what she was doing and stood still.

"How could he say that?" Charlotte cried.

"He needs his taste buds looked at," Louis snapped.

Naveen raised up his hand. "Wait," he said. "Let me finish!" He glanced down at the paper and continued to read. "'Princess Tiana's gumbo was even better than my granddaddy's!'"

Tiana dropped her spoon. "Could you read that again?" she asked. She couldn't believe her ears!

"You heard correctly," Naveen said, grinning. But he reread the line and the rest of the glowing review. "'Like the jewels in a royal tiara, this restaurant is a precious jewel in New Orleans. Tiana's Palace earns five stars. It is la crème de la crème!'"

Everyone rushed over and hugged Tiana.

"What a lovely review!" her mother exclaimed. "I knew that he couldn't resist your cooking. Congratulations, Tiana."

"Well deserved." Charlotte beamed.

"I knew he would love it," Louis added.

Naveen folded up the newspaper. "I'd say this calls for a beignet celebration," he cried. "First batch ready?"

Tiana laughed. "Coming right up!" she said. She placed the fresh-cooked pastries on a platter and sprinkled some powdered sugar over them. It was a royal feast!

The phone rang, and Charlotte answered.

"What, you want a table for tonight?" she said. "Let me see if we have anything."

Tiana looked at her friend worriedly.

Didn't Lottie know they didn't have any reservations yet?

Charlotte winked at her. "It looks like we can squeeze you in around six forty-five," she said.

"What were you doing, Lottie?" Tiana asked as soon as her friend hung up.

"I was just making sure they knew it wouldn't be easy to get a reservation here. After all, it's a jewel of New Orleans." The phone rang and Charlotte grinned. "See?"

"Sounds like other folks are reading the review!" Naveen exclaimed.

"I think that you're going to be very busy around here," her mother sang out.

Laughing, Tiana nodded her head. Just as Charlotte had said, many people listened to Jono La Crème's opinions about what restaurants were good. Since he gave her a five-star royal review, everyone in town wanted to come! And the more people who wanted to come to Tiana's Palace, the better!

Naveen picked up Tiana and twirled her

around the kitchen. "Well, Princess Tiana, what do you have to say?"

Tiana's eyes sparkled. "This is the best palace in the world. A place where everyone will come to have a royally good time."

With a beignet in hand, Tiana toasted her friends and family. "To a royal success," she said.

Everyone laughed and then enjoyed the most delicious beignets in New Orleans.

Don't miss the next enchanting Disney Princess chapter book!

Jasmine
The
Missing
Coin

*L*ife at the palace is splendid for Princess Jasmine and Prince Aladdin! With Aladdin's birthday coming up, Jasmine wants to find him the perfect gift. So she sets off on the Magic Carpet with Rajah the tiger. She is determined to track down the camel coin Aladdin is missing from his rare-coin collection. It's smooth sailing until Magic Carpet suddenly loses its power, stranding Jasmine and Rajah in the desert! Will they ever find the special coin and make it back to the palace in time for Aladdin's birthday?